This book should be returned to any branch of the
Lancashire County Library on or before the date shown

0 4 MAY 2019

1 9 AUG 2019

- 7 DEC 2019

Lancashire County Library,
County Hall Complex,
1st floor Christ Church Precinct,
Preston, PR1 8XJ

Lancashire
County
Council

www.lancashire.gov.uk/libraries

LL1 (A)

$$t(x^2) \div \sqrt{9\, y(x)} = p4^2(x)$$

$$4.729 - 1.3(x^2) \times \frac{6}{4}(y^6) = x\left(\frac{1}{3}\right)$$

$x + c/2$

$CH_2\,COOH$

$$fct\ \frac{y\left(\frac{6+9}{2}\right)\frac{4}{2} - \frac{x}{3}}{r(3\frac{x}{2}) + 9}$$

864
792
46
420

$a^3 +$

$(x-j^2$

$fct\ \sqrt{6}$

0

a
b
c
e
h

$c^2 - sinh(x)$

tr

This paperback edition first published in
Great Britain in 2018 by Andersen Press Ltd.
First published in Great Britain in 2017
by Andersen Press Ltd.,
20 Vauxhall Bridge Road, London SW1V 2SA.
Text copyright © Kathryn White, 2017.
Illustrations copyright © Adrian Reynolds, 2017.
The rights of Kathryn White and Adrian Reynolds
to be identified as the author and illustrator of
this work have been asserted by them in accordance
with the Copyright, Designs and Patents Act, 1988.
All rights reserved. Printed and bound in Malaysia.
10 9 8 7 6 5 4 3 2 1
British Library Cataloguing in Publication Data available.
ISBN 978 1 78344 589 9

FOR ARTHUR, SYLVIA AND FRIDA KATHRYN, THREE BEAUTIFUL BABIES - K.W   FOR ARCHIE AND ELLA - A.R

THE TICKLE TEST

Kathryn White

Adrian Reynolds

It's easy to **tickle** a tall giraffe,

she'll **giggle** and **gurgle** and chuckle and laugh.

And it's certainly fun  to tickle

a BEAR,
he'll jiggle and wriggle and bounce everywhere.

That gave me a scare!

An octopus
loves to be tickled for sure,

but which was the arm
that I tickled before?

To tickle a tiger,
hide under
his knees,

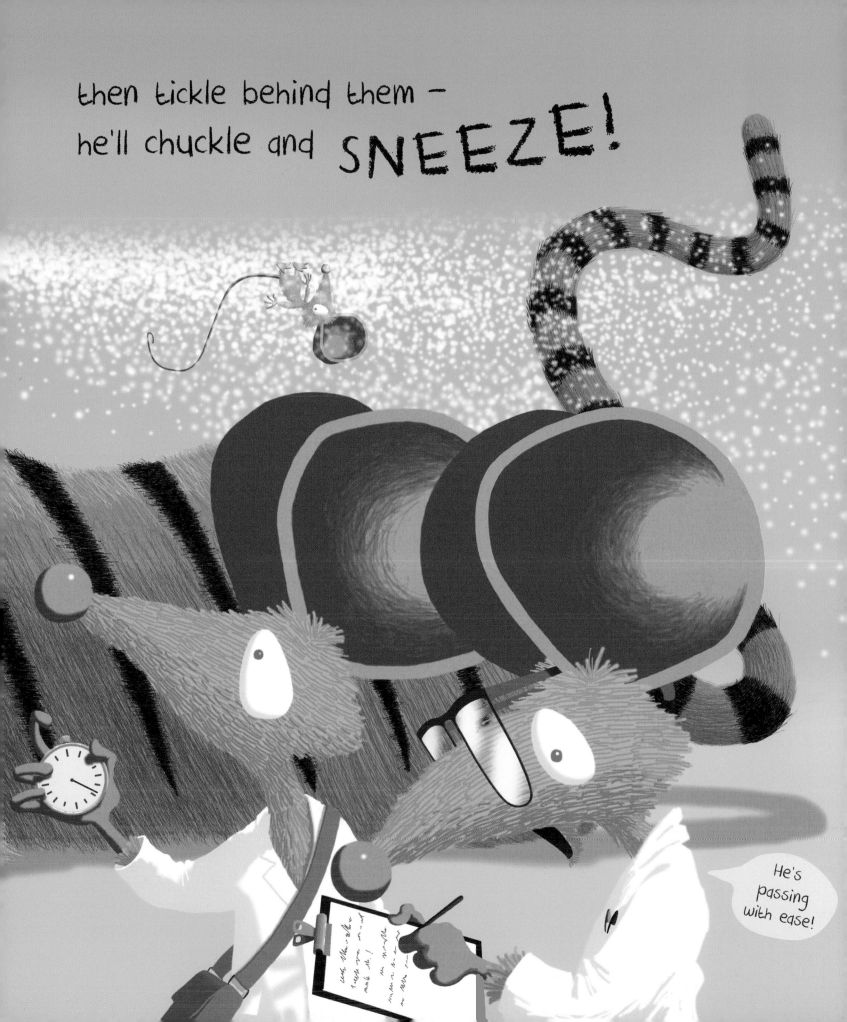

Creep up and tickle
an elephant's toes.

Beware

bottom trumpets –
hold your nose!

Flamingos adore just a tickle or two
but watch out for feathers or they'll tickle you.

And how to tickle a crocodile?
This dangerous test needs timing and style.

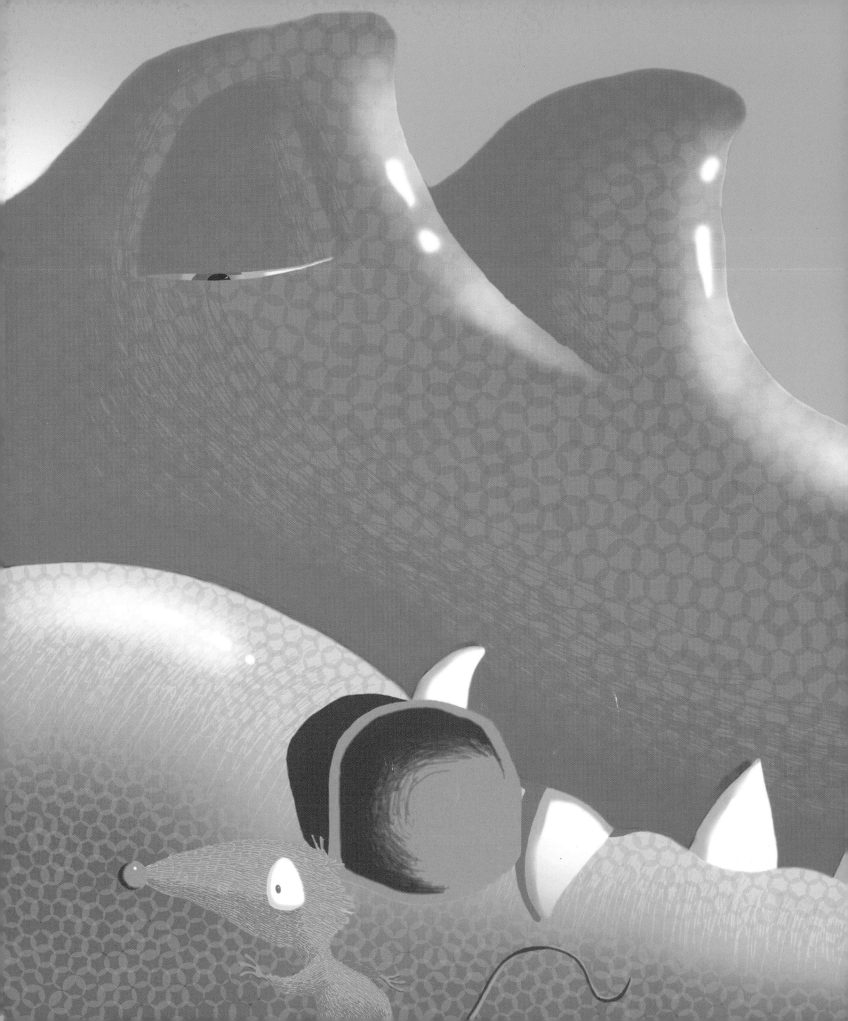

If crocodile spies you,
then you'd better dash –
those sharp teeth will
gobble you up in a flash!

he'll hoot with delight,
as he does with his mummy!
Tickling and laughing
are such fun to do.

So please tell us
just where we
should tickle...

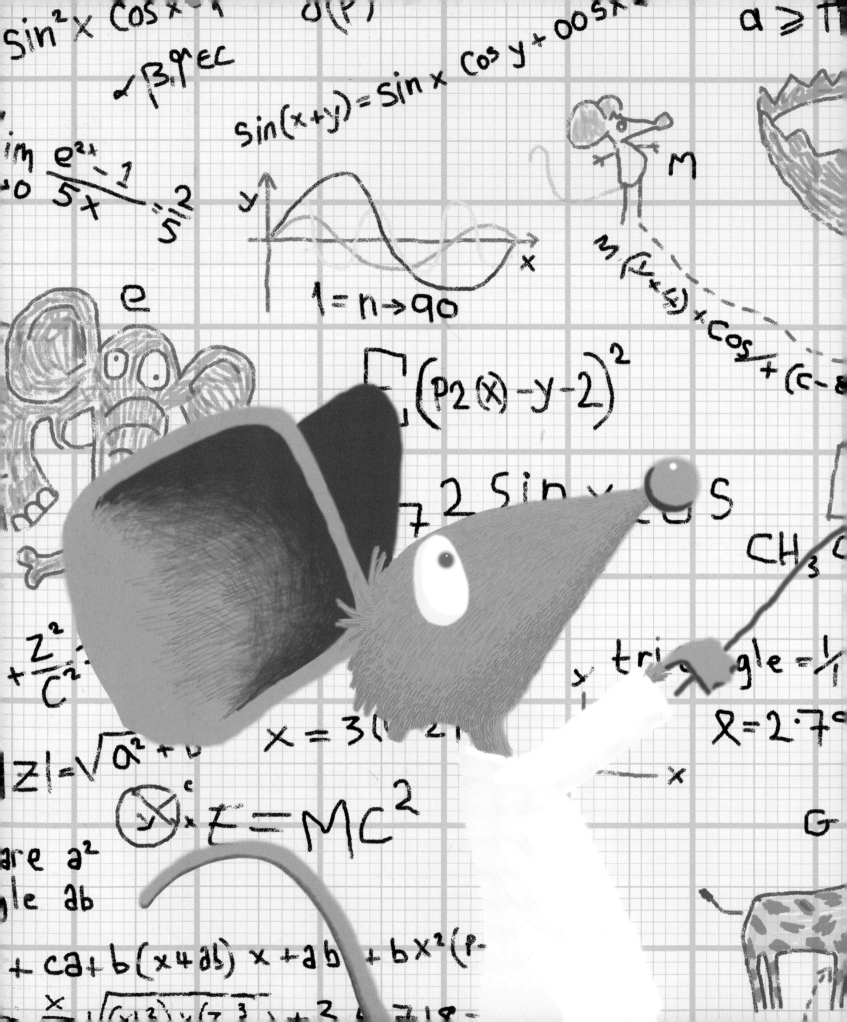

$$t(x^2) \div \sqrt{9\, y(x)} = \beta 4^2(x)$$

a

b

e

h

c

c

$$4.729 - 1.3(x^2) \times \frac{6}{4}(y^4) = x\left(\frac{1}{3}\right)$$

$x = c/2$

864
792
46
420
c

$CH_2 \, COOH$

$(x - j$

$fct \, \sqrt{6}$

0

$$fct \; \frac{y\left(\frac{6+9}{2}\right)\frac{4}{2} \cdot \frac{x}{3}}{r\left(3 \times \frac{1}{2}\right) + 9}$$

$a^3 +$

$b^2 = (\ldots) r a^2 - ab)$

B

$+\!\!\!/_6$ A

m

$c^2 = \sinh(x)$

tr